MW00954771

a day in
RICETOWN

A RICEMONSTER COLOURING AND ACTIVITY BOOK

Thames & Hudson

MEET THE RICEMONSTERS

 Say hello to Ricecracker and his friends.

Ricemon

is very brave, he is always o an adventure.

Ricecracker

is sweet and kind, he is everyone's friend.

Miss Dino

is super happy! She likes to laugh and play.

Ricepuffy

is always sleepy. She likes cuddles and ice cream.

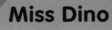

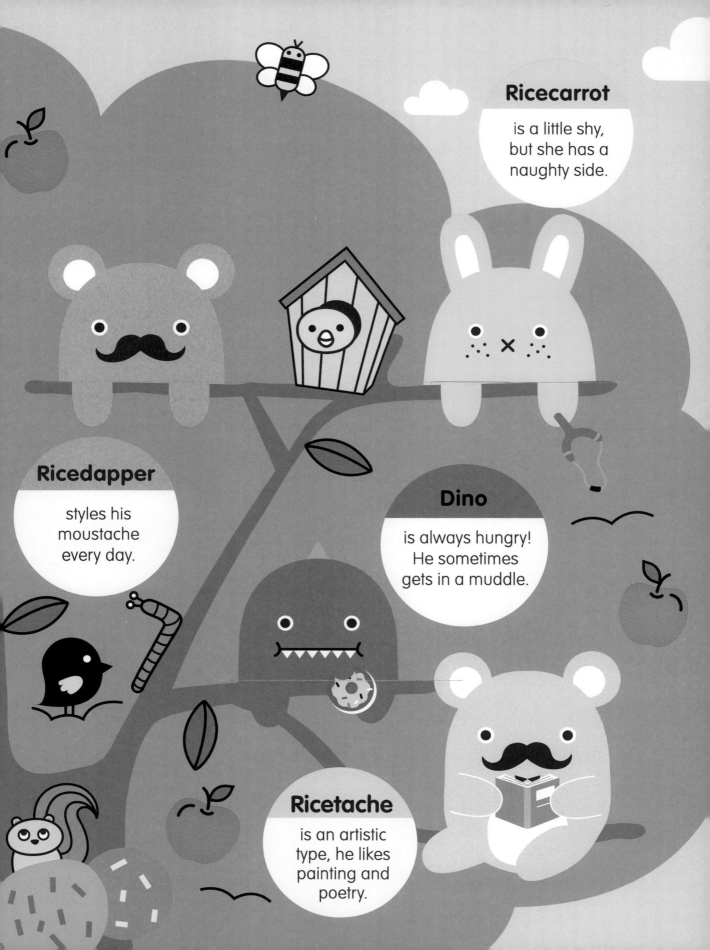

Ricecarrot

is a little shy, but she has a naughty side.

Ricedapper

styles his moustache every day.

Dino

is always hungry! He sometimes gets in a muddle.

Ricetache

is an artistic type, he likes painting and poetry.

HOW TO USE THIS BOOK...

▷ DECORATE

Decorate the blank puppets to create
new characters. Draw yourself on a
puppet to become part of the story!

▷ SLOT

Slide the puppets into the slots on
each page to add them to the story
and to complete the activities.

▷ DRAW

Draw on the pages to give your
puppets new looks. Add hats,
outfits or new hairstyles.

COMPLETE

Draw beneath the slots to complete outfits, chairs, or vehicles for puppets to sit in.

PUT AWAY

When you've finished playing put us back in our safe space!

MAKE MORE PUPPETS

To create more blank puppets to draw on, simply trace around the existing puppets and cut out.

Tell me more about you.

THIS BOOK BELONGS TO:

This is me!

I LIVE IN:

Pop your puppet here and draw your friends and family in the windows.

Draw your room here.

WELCOME TO RICETOWN

This is Ricetown, home of the Ricemonsters. Today is Ricecracker's birthday! Help Ricecracker and his friends get ready for his big party.

OFF WE GO!

It's nearly party time!
How are you getting there?
Draw your own car or
choose your wheels.

Draw
your own
cars.

FIND RICEMON'S HAT

Ricemon needs his hat for the fancy dress party but his room is a little bit messy. Can you help him find his hat?

It looks like this:

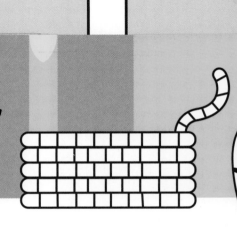
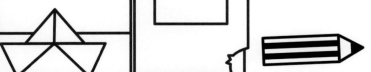

TIME TO PLAY

The Ricemonsters visit the park on the way. Who wants to go on the seesaw with Ricecracker?

IN THE SCULPTURE GARDEN

Some of the statues are missing.
Perhaps the Ricemonsters can help.

Can you draw the missing statues?

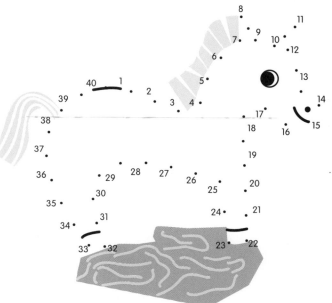

8
7
6
5
40 1
2
3 4
39
38
37
36
35
34
33 32
31
30
29 28 27 26
25
24 23 22
21
20
19
18
17
16
15
14
13
12
11
10
9

What statue is hidden here? Finish the dot-to-dot.

RICETACHE'S ART GALLERY

▷ **Ricetache forgot the party was today! Quickly help him fill his gallery with pictures.**

You look picture perfect.

Draw a self-portrait.

Sit on me!

GOING SWIMMING

Time for a quick dip. Let's cool off in the lake! Colour in all the fish.

RICEPUFFY'S ICE CREAM VAN

You can't have a birthday without ice cream. Ricepuffy knows every Ricemonster's favourite flavour. What's yours?

Oh no, your ice cream!

RICETOWN HIGH STREET

It's time to pick up the party supplies.
Which shops will you visit?

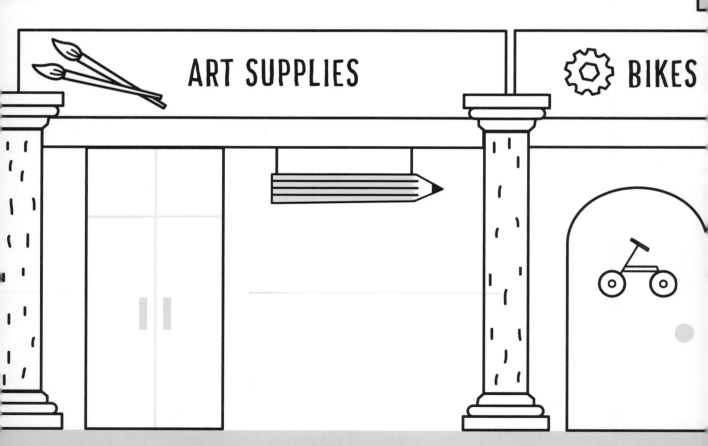

ART SUPPLIES

BIKES

PARTY STORE

Fill the shop windows with fun things.

RICEDAPPER'S BARBER SHOP

Welcome to Ricedapper's barber shop. Try out new looks for the Ricemonsters here.

WAITING AREA

TAKE A SEAT

Draw me a cool new hairstyle.

Would you mind helping me style my moustache?

NOO-MOUSTACHE WAX

Slot your
puppet here
to try out
the wigs.

Try
me
too!

What style
would you
like today?

AT THE MARKET

The Ricemonsters stop by the market to buy some fruit and veggies. Can you spot the odd things out?

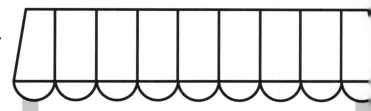

Please fill the market stalls!

Hide a Ricemonster in the trolley.

MISS DINO'S SWEET SHOP

Miss Dino is coming to the party. She's bringing lots of yummy sweets. Which are your favourite?

Please help fill all the sweet jars!

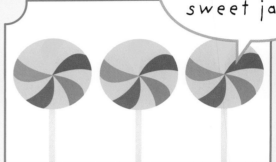

SWEET COUNTER

Draw flowers.

See you at the party!

Design Miss Dino's shop sign.

RICECARROT'S GARDEN

Ricecarrot is coming to the party.
Can you guess her favourite vegetable?

Who's looking out
of the window?

Draw
Ricecarrot's
plants.

Who lives in
this nest?

What's growing in
this patch? Is it animal,
vegetable or mineral?

Draw some
more bugs.

 # ON THE BUS

The Ricemonsters have everything they need for the party. Let's get the bus to Ricecracker's house.

Fill the bus with passengers.

DINO'S BALLOONS

Uh-oh, poor Dino has got himself into a knotty situation! Put Ricemonsters in the slots. Who is holding each balloon?

Knot again...

Place a puppet in each cloud and decorate a balloon to match.

Find the end of each balloon's string.

DECORATE RICECRACKER'S HOUSE

Help the Ricemonsters get the house ready for the party. Paint the sign, hang up balloons and colour the bunting.

HAPPY BIRTHDAY RICECRACKER!

What a lot of presents!
Complete the dot-to-dots
to see what they are.

Would you like a piece of cake?

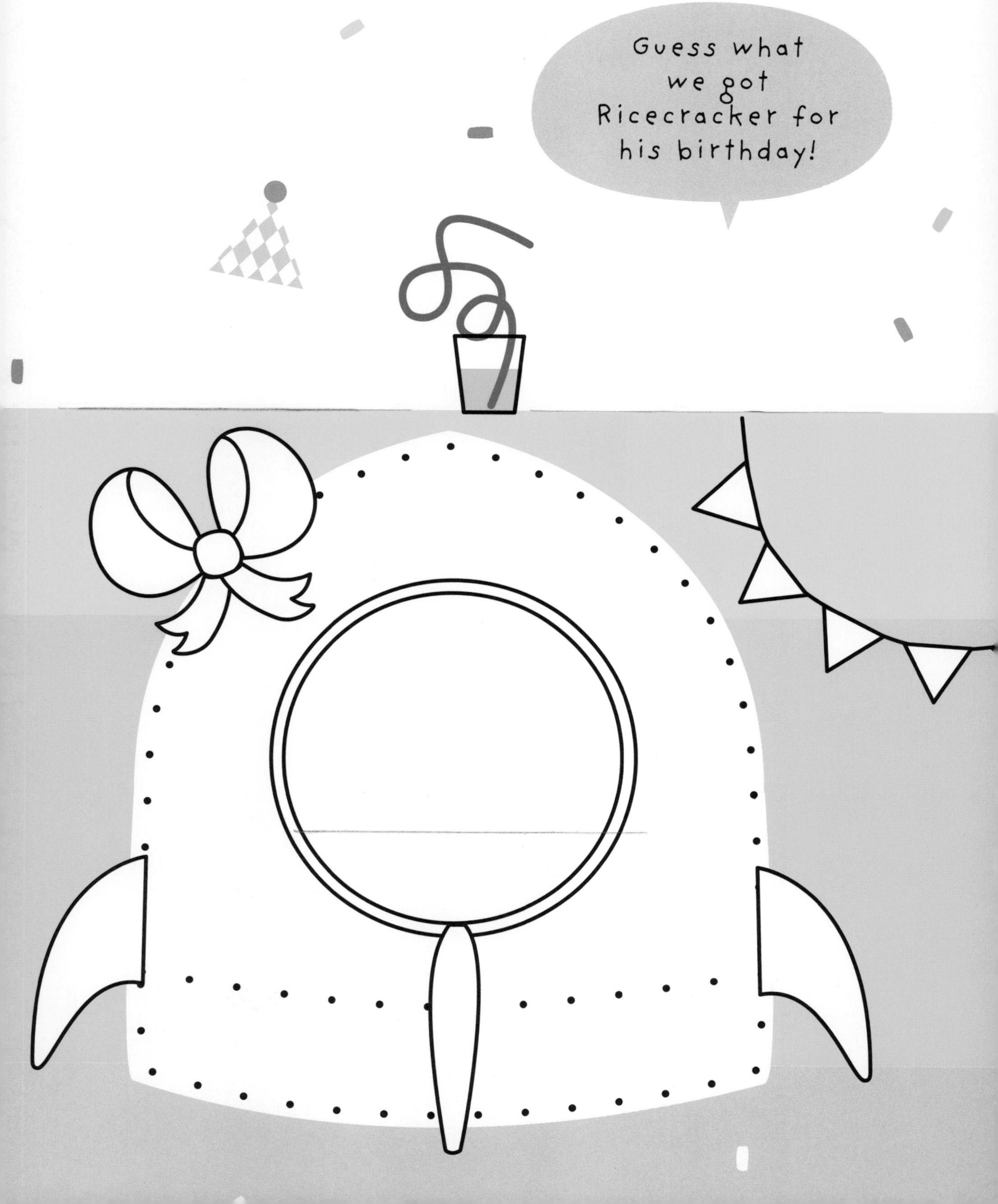
Guess what we got Ricecracker for his birthday!

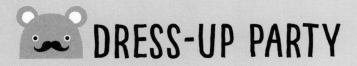

DRESS-UP PARTY

Fancy dress parties are the best!
Help the Ricemonsters dress up.

Draw, colour and complete the outfits.

LET'S DANCE

Time to boogie! Draw party clothes for the Ricemonsters on the dance floor.

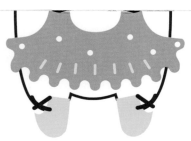

This is my favourite song!

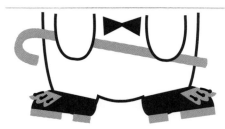

I'm a disco diva.

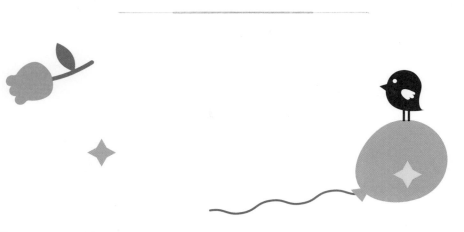

GOODNIGHT!

After such a wonderful day, it's time
for the Ricemonsters to go to sleep...

Put each Ricemonster to bed.

HAPPY MEMORIES

Draw yourself into the photos as a reminder of the fun you had in Ricetown!